TOO BUSY MARCO

Roz Chast

atheneum books for young readers
new york london toronto sydney

ATHENEUM BOOKS FOR YOUNG READERS
An imprint of Simon & Schuster Children's Publishing Division
1230 Avenue of the Americas, New York, New York 10020
For information about special discounts for bulk purchases, please contact Simon & Schuster Special Sales
at 1-866-506-1949 or business@simonandschuster.com.
The Simon & Schuster Speakers Bureau can bring authors to your live event.
For more information or to book an event, contact the Simon & Schuster Speakers Bureau
at 1-866-248-3049 or visit our website at www.simonspeakers.com.
Book design by Lizzy Bromley
The text for this book is set in Edlund.
The illustrations for this book are rendered in watercolor and gouache.
Manufactured in China
0610 SCP
First Edition
2 4 6 8 10 9 7 5 3 1
Library of Congress Cataloging-in-Publication Data
Chast, Roz.
Too busy Marco / Roz Chast. — 1st ed.
p. cm.
Summary: Marco the bird does not want to take the time to prepare for bedtime
because there are so many more important things for him to do.
ISBN 978-1-4169-8474-0 (hardcover)
[1. Birds—Fiction. 2. Bedtime—Fiction. 3. Humorous stories.] I. Title.
PZ7.C3877To 2010
[E]—dc22
2009052481

To the real Marco

Once again, it was time for Marco to go to bed.

But Marco didn't WANT to go to bed.
He didn't have TIME for bed. He had . . .

He still had to paint his masterpiece.

. . . discover new fish!

Maybe he could work on his paintings underwater.

Naturally he would need to invent underwater paint.

Not a problem! He was good at inventing things.

Like . . .

THE STILT CAR

THE STRATOSPHERIC BOUNCING BALL

THE DREAM RECORDER

and . . . Invisibility Gum.

Everyone would want some.
He would become famous.

And when he'd get tired from all that serious work,
he could relax by skateboarding.

Marco, aren't you forgetting about something?

So that settled it. He would be a deep-sea-diving

What about his uncle Ed?
Uncle Ed *bowled* for a living!

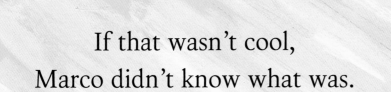

If that wasn't cool,
Marco didn't know what was.

There was nothing about bowling he didn't like.

The different-colored bowling balls . . .   The sound of pins being knocked down . . .

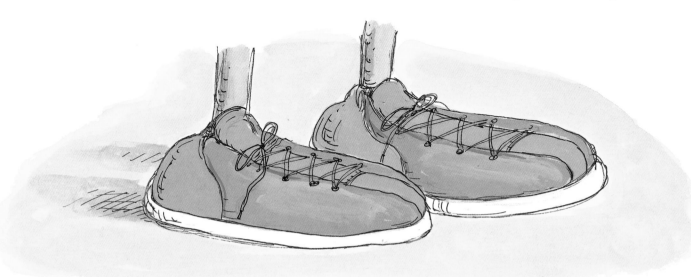

The way the shoes felt on his claws . . .

This was getting very complicated.

How could he do it all?

Couldn't he have just FIVE

TEENY-TINY

eentsy-weentsy

BITSY — WITSY

SMALL, LITTLE, MINIATURE

MICROSCOPIC, SHRIMPY, MEASLY

MINUTES?!?

Who could go to bed when . . .

there were trampoline-jumping records to be broken?

Wasn't practicing the banjo just a little bit more important than bedtime?

Get down from there, Marco.

How could someone brush their beak when they would much rather be climbing Mt. Everest . . .

. . . or flying in a spaceship and discovering space monkeys . . .